MIKE YOUNG

SUPERTED
AND THE SPACE BEAVERS

ADAPTED BY MAUREEN SPURGEON

ILLUSTRATIONS FROM ANIMATED DESIGNS
BY DAVE EDWARDS

CARNIVAL

Nobody saw Dr Freezing Frost arrive. One moment it was a quiet, peaceful morning in the forest . . . And, the next? There he was at the wheel of a huge, noisy machine. "I prescribe," he roared, "that we plough down the forest with perfect precision!"

Pengy, the Penguin Man, gave a snigger. He knew what the doctor was planning . . .

But ploughing down a forest wasn't that easy. No matter which way the doctor tried to go, his machine bounced from tree to tree - like an enormous pinball machine. Then, with a loud BANG! it crashed.

"Yeeeaaah!" screamed Dr Frost as he and Pengy landed head-first, right in the holes of a giant tree trunk.

Now, SuperTed and his friend, Spottyman, lived in a tree house. But on that particular day they had something else to worry about. After all, what would *you* say if you were reading your favourite comic, and a chair leg broke off?

"Woooah!" cried SuperTed, crashing to the floor.

"Great moons of the planet Spot!" gasped Spotty, his great spotty eyes widening. "That chair leg's making for the door. It's got a mind of its own!"

"Worse than that, Spotty," cried SuperTed. "It's got termites!" He made a desperate grab. "Give that back!"

But those termites put up such a fight for the chair leg, Spottyman knew there was only one creature in the universe to beat them - the dreaded Space Beavers, who could chew through whole forests.

Dr Frost had heard of the Space
Beavers too . . .

Nothing could stop a Space Beaver
chomping away at a tree for long. Not
even a flashing sign which said:

> COME TO EARTH.
> OPEN ALL NIGHT.
> 31 TREE-LICIOUS FLAVOURS!

But Space Beaver Wally and his pal,
The Beav, slowed down just long
enough to lick their lips.

"Can we go, Wally?" slurped The
Beav, looking forward to a real feast.

"Sure, why not?" said Wally, gulping
down the last mouthfull. "Let's tell the
rest of the gang!"

Dr Frost and Pengy were already waiting as the beaver-tail rocket landed - right next to their ice-cream fortress at the South Pole.

"Salutations, Space Beavers," the doctor greeted. "Are you hungry?"

"We sure are, Mister!" nodded The Beav, eagerly smacking his lips.

"Earth is filled with delectable deciduous delights," smiled the doctor, showing them a map. "Munch to your heart's content!" He scribbled a note and held it out to The Beav. "I give you my written permission."

"Thanks a lot, Mister!" shouted Wally, dashing back to the beaver-tail rocket. "Come on, Beav!"

"And now, Pengy," murmered Dr Frost, "I will show you my wonderfully wicked weather machine . . ."

No wonder there were three snowmen on guard, Pengy thought, following on behind. It was certainly an impressive contraption. Dr Frost's cold eyes glittered.

"After the beavers level all the trees," he was saying, "I'll flood the Earth! Then I'll set the thermostat to REAL COLD and cover it with ice. We can stage our trans-global ice ballet!"

SuperTed knew nothing about all
this. He and Spotty were too busy
getting rid of the termites.

They had hardly finished that job
when two very frightened squirrels
burst in through the front door,
chattering. SuperTed looked alarmed.
"He says they're eating everything in
sight, Spotty!"

"Impossible!" Spottyman patted the
bulging cleaner. "They're in the bag."

"Not the termites!" shouted
SuperTed. "Space Beavers! They're
eating the whole forest and scaring off
all the woodland creatures."

Spotty sighed and reached for his rocket pack. "SuperTed," he said, "you'd better say your secret magic word."

Next moment, in a flash of red and gold, SuperTed was flying through the air with Spottyman right behind him.

As soon as he caught sight of the Space Beavers, SuperTed roared, "Stop chewing, NOW! These trees don't belong to you!"

"Yes they do," protested The Beav, with bulging cheeks. "Dr Freezing Frost wrote us a note."

"Dr Frost?" echoed SuperTed, scornfully. "That cold creep?"

"He's not a creep," retorted The Beav. "He's giving us free eats!"

"So that makes you lot the creeps!" finished Wally. "Let's get 'em, gang!"

SuperTed and Spotty only just managed to duck out of the way as a giant log came hurtling towards them!

"Jump!" shouted SuperTed, as the log approached like a steamroller. "And keep back-pedalling!"

"They'll never make it up that steep hill," roared Wally. But SuperTed and Spottyman did not give up that easily.

"Hey!" yelled The Beav. "Come on down so we can flatten you!"

"Okay!" SuperTed shouted back. "If that's what you want."

They turned and rolled back down the hill towards the beavers, now going at ten times the speed.

"Let's roll them out of the forest, SuperTed!" cried Spotty.

They might have succeeded, too, if the log hadn't crashed into the rocks and shot them high into the air!

"Fire up your rocket pack, Spotty!" shouted SuperTed.

Too late! Wally and The Beav were already using their tails as bats, hitting up the largest rocks they could find, making SuperTed and Spotty hurtle to the ground.

And all this time, Dr Freezing Frost
was punching lots of buttons on his
weather machine.

"The Space Beavers should be
finished, Pengy," he beamed. "Now,
storm clouds such as civilization has
never seen are circulating over every
centimetre of this sphere!"

He pressed a remote control button
to reveal his rocket ship. "Come,
Pengy," said Dr Frost. "World
conquest and our ice ballet awaits."

Dr Frost was right about the rain. SuperTed and Spotty were already soaked.

SuperTed decided the time had come to try one last, desperate trick. "I'm the law around here," he told the beavers. "So you'd better come along quietly!"

"Cream them, Pengy!" interrupted a voice, and a hand pulled the trigger on the spine-chilling splurge-gun.

"Yuck!" shuddered Spotty, first to get hit. "This is disgusting!"

"No it isn't," answered SuperTed, taking a lick. "It's tutti-frutti!"

"Tie them to a log," growled Dr Frost. "Then toss these trouble-makers into the river!"

There was a lot of huffing and puffing, a loud splash, and then SuperTed and Spotty vanished into the swirling waters.

"I - I can't loosen the ropes, SuperTed," panted Spottyman.

"Keep trying!" came the order. "D'you want us to dive straight over the dam?"

But it was impossible. Down, down, down fell the log, with SuperTed and Spotty being sucked into the river. By some miracle they came to the surface - but even more danger lay ahead!

With so much rain from Dr Frost's machine, the river had overflowed its banks. Great boulders were toppling in the water.

"Great moons of Spot!" cried Spotty. "We're going to be bashed, SuperTed!"

"Hold still, Spotty," yelled SuperTed, kicking as hard as he could. "I'll use my rocket boots to burn your ropes."

How Spotty managed to keep calm long enough, he never knew.

"Just like cutting butter with a blowtorch!" was SuperTed's verdict.

Spotty untied SuperTed with only seconds to spare, before the log smashed into a gigantic boulder. Still the nightmare continued, with the river thrashing and tossing them about until they finally reached land.

And that was when they were greeted by a voice they knew only too well . . .

"Hey Wally - there are those trouble-makers again!"

"Let's take care of them for good, Beav!"

For a moment, SuperTed and Spottyman stood quite still. They could hardly believe that there was only one tree standing. Slowly it toppled to the ground.

"Look what you've done!" choked SuperTed. "You've chewed down an entire forest!"

A loud CRACK! made them whirl around. Water was gushing through an enormous split in the dam, and it was becoming wider and wider!

"Floundering fruitcakes!" shouted SuperTed. "It's a tidal wave!"

A giant wall of water crashed down.

SuperTed, Spottyman and the beavers clung on to bushes and stumps of trees - but Wally and The Beav were not so lucky.

SuperTed heard their cries for help as they were dragged underwater once, then twice, each time struggling to the surface and gasping for air.

Suddenly SuperTed gave a cry. "There they are! Come on, Spotty!" Together they flew into the air, hovering above the surging river.

The Beav was the first to be rescued, hauled out of the water by SuperTed. Then Spotty dived in. "Thank goodness!" he spluttered, bringing Wally to the surface. "They're okay!"

By this time, all the Space Beavers were cheering - all except Wally and The Beav, who were still out of breath.

"That was really neat," Wally panted.

"Whatever can we do to repay you?" spluttered The Beav.

"Promise not to chew up any more forests!" said SuperTed at once.

They had hardly shaken hands on the deal when there was a deafening series of screams. Hundreds of people were running for cover! The wall of water was surging towards a stream which ran through a canyon leading right into their town.

"We've got to stop that water," commanded SuperTed in a loud voice. "And we'll need your help, beavers!"

This time The Beav and Wally worked as hard as anyone, floating logs up the stream, moving them in any way they could.

"That's great!" shouted SuperTed,
flying up and putting another log on
top of the hundreds already piled up to
make a dam. "Keep them coming! We
don't have much time!"

And SuperTed was right. He had
hardly put the last log in place, when
the river gushed towards the dam.

Everyone held their breath as the
water hit the logs with a thundering
crash. There was a great shudder.
But, the dam held firm.

"It worked!" cried SuperTed.

"Yaaaayyyy!" yelled the beavers.

"Thank goodness *that's* all over with!" said Spotty.

SuperTed became serious again. "What about Dr Frost?" he said. And even as he spoke, Dr Freezing Frost was lowering the temperature on his wicked weather machine!

By now people were coming out into the streets, cheering, "We're safe! Hurray for SuperTed!"

They began linking arms to dance on the wet pavements. But not for long . . .

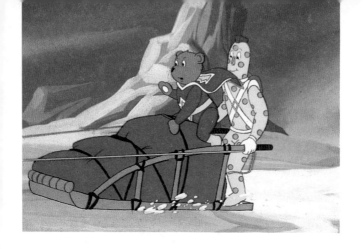

"Yeeaaah!" screamed The Beav and Wally, slipping and sliding on the ice. "Whoooaaah!"

"Spotted Sputniks!" gasped Spotty, as giant ice balls began hailing down. Weather reports started coming in.

"Raging Niagara Falls freezes!"

"Joggers in Manchester freeze in mid-step!"

"The Sahara Desert is as slippery as . . . well, ice!"

Meanwhile, SuperTed and Spotty were on their way to the South Pole. Their sledge, pulled by a team of Space Beavers, slid to a halt as Dr Frost's fortress came in sight.

Getting inside would be no problem, SuperTed thought. He was sure that he and Spotty could be wonderful ice-cream men - until one of the snowmen sentries shouted, "Halt! Imposters!"

In an instant, SuperTed and Spotty fired up their rocket boots and rocket pack, melting all the snowmen's feet.

Next minute, those same feet froze, holding the snowmen fast to the icy ground, powerless to move.

"Freeze!" roared a voice, and Dr Frost and Pengy appeared, armed with ice blasters shooting icy blue rays.

"Mirror, mirror on the wall . . ." muttered SuperTed, grabbing the nearest one, "bounce these rays back down the hall!"

His idea worked perfectly! The first ray bounced off the mirror, turning Pengy into a giant icicle!

Dr Frost was furious! "Another turn of the knob!" he raged, lunging for his weather machine, "and the world becomes a Winter Wasteland!"

"Yuck!" Suddenly his hand was splattered with gooey ice-cream! "What's this?"

"Your just desserts, Dr Frost!" cried SuperTed. By the time he and the others had finished, the enemy looked like a human banana split!"

"Now for the weather machine, gang!" yelled SuperTed. "It's twenty years in the cooler for Dr Frost!"

With Dr Frost well and truly beaten, the Space Beavers were soon enjoying themselves, helping SuperTed and Spotty replant the forest.

Everyone was sad when the time came for them to return to the beaver-tail rocket ship. "Goodbye!" shouted Wally and The Beav.

"Let's go home, Spotty," yawned SuperTed, stretching himself. "I'm exhausted!" But the excitement was not over yet . . .